Science Fun with Water and Ice

Toni S. Gould and Marie Warnke

Illustrations by Paulette Rich Long

Walker and Company ☀ **New York**

First published in the United States of America
in 1983 by the Walker Publishing Company, Inc.

Published simultaneously in Canada by John Wiley & Sons
Canada, Limited, Rexdale, Ontario.

ISBN: 0-8027-9192-1

Library of Congress Catalog Card Number: 83-5938

Printed in the United States of America

10 9 8 7 6 5 4 3 2 1

Library of Congress Cataloging in Publication Data

Gould, Toni S.
  Science fun with water and ice.

  (A Learn to read book ; 4)
  Summary: Presents a variety of facts, simple
experiments, and jokes and tricks involving water and
ice; a description of Antarctica; and brief biographies
of Diana Nyad and Beth Heiden.
  1. Water—Juvenile literature. 2. Ice—Juvenile
literature. [1. Water. 2. Ice] 1. Warnke, Marie.
II. Long, Paulette Rich, ill. III. Title. IV. Series:
Gould, Toni S. Learn to read book ; 4.
GB662.3.G68 1983   546'.22   83-5938
ISBN 0-8027-9192-1

CONTENTS

Scope and Sequence Chart for Set IV

variant long vowels

Title	Focus	Study Words	Language Concepts
1. Fun Facts	soft *c* and *g*	water, nothing, or, once, does, giant, more	degree sign (°), Fahrenheit (F)
2. Things to Do with Water and Ice	*ay, ee*	lighter, bottle, out	fraction (½)
3. Fun and Games with Water and Ice	*ea, oa*	should, would, needle, paper, flour, elephant, could, salt	————
4. A Land of Ice and Snow	*ai, ow, ue*	Antarctica, never, iceberg, color, penguin, cover, women, world	paragraph indenting
5. Diana Nyad	*īe, ew,* schwa *a*	Diana Nyad, before, until, Olympics, distance, New York, ever	time (5:30)
6. Eric and Beth Heiden	single long vowels	Eric Heiden, grandma, gym, doctor, won, Dianne Holum, third, medal	————

Fun Facts

Focus: soft *c* and *g*

Water is everywhere. Sometimes, when it's very cold, we see it as ice. Sometimes, when it's very hot, we can't see it! Then water becomes a gas.

We must have water.

Every living thing must have water. Too little water can make us sick. So can too much water. Living things are made of many cells. Since cells are so little, we can not see just one.

Every cell in us is made up of a lot of water. If we eat nothing for a month, we can still live. But, if we stop drinking, we will get sick very fast.

Where does ice come from?

When it gets very, very cold, fresh water changes to ice. A very long time ago, men went to a lake or pond after it had changed to ice. They cut the ice into big blocks.

Then they put the ice on sleds and pulled it home. They kept the ice in an ice shed so that they had ice when it was hot.

Fish in a pond.

Sometimes the ice at the top of a pond can be thick.
Sometimes it can be thin. If the pond is filled only with ice,
fish can not live in it. If there is space under the ice, fish can
live.

In some ponds, you have to catch the fish with nets when it gets cold. Then you must put them in tanks inside so they can live.

Help yourself to an ice pack!

Can you think of a time when you fell? Can you think what it felt like? What did you do to help yourself? Once you get a bump, cut, or scrape, the best thing to do is to get an ice pack. But, don't put just ice on the cut.

You can buy an ice pack. Or, you can make one with ice cubes. Just put ice in a face cloth. Place this ice pack on the cut, the bump, or the scrape till the swelling stops.

Frostbite

Does it get very cold where you live? If you don't dress for the cold, you can get frostbite. A "biting" cold is less than 10°F. If the winds are strong and it is damp, you can get frostbite when it is only 32°F.

You get frostbite when the water in your skin cells changes to ice. The skin gets red and then white. If you don't get help, the cells will be killed by the ice. The best help is to put warm, not hot, water on the skin at once. Do not rub the skin. Don't let your hands and face get too cold since these are the places where kids get frostbite.

Water can crack rocks!

Can water be stronger than rocks? Water drops hit giant rocks like a gun shot. Water gets into the cracks. When it gets cold, the water changes to ice.

The ice in the cracks can split the rocks. The water drops hit the rocks for a very long time. This can make the rocks flat. The rocks that get cracked by the ice can sometimes make a landslide.

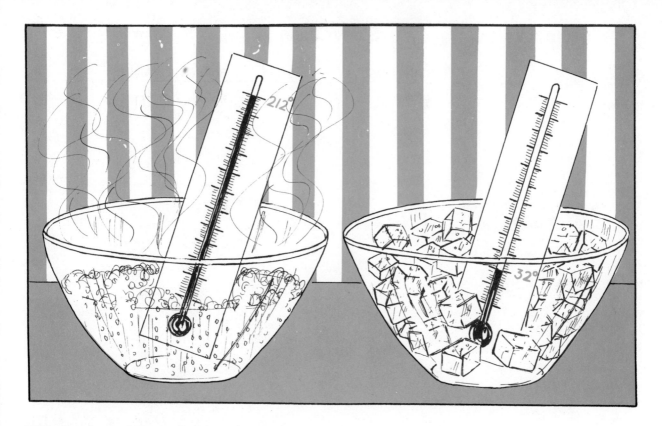

Water and ice facts.

Water and ice have no taste and no smell. Look at the top of this page. Water changes to gas at 212°F. Water changes to ice at 32°F. Water takes up more space when it changes to ice. If you live by the water, it will be warmer than if you don't.

Study Guide

soft *c* words	soft *g* words	new study words
ice	change	water
since	page	nothing
cell		or
space		once
face		does
place		giant
		more

Language Concepts: degree sign (°), Fahrenheit (F)

Things to Do with Water and Ice

Focus: *ay, ee*

Can water cut up a pen?

You will need: 2 glasses, 2 pens, and water.

Fill only one glass with water. Put the pens in the glasses.

Look at the pens from every side of the glasses. What do you see?

The pen in the glass with water seems to have been cut in two. The pen in the glass with no water still looks like one pen.

Where can the water be?

You will need: 2 little plates and water.

Put water in the plates. The water must be the same in the two plates. Place one plate in the sun. Place one plate in the shade. Check the plates in two, maybe three days. What do you see?

The plate left in the sun has no water. The plate in the shade has only a little water left. The more sun, the faster the water changes into a gas.

Where does the water go?

You will need: 2 glasses the same size, 1 lid, and water. Put a line ½ way up the two glasses. Fill the glasses with water up to the lines. Put a lid on one glass. Place the two glasses in the sun. Check the glasses in three days. What do you see?

In the glass with the lid, the [water is at] the line. In the glass with no lid, some wat[er is l]ost. The sun has changed some water into [vapor. It] went up from the glass.

What will the rag feel like?

You will need: a rag, a freezer, and water.

Wet the rag. Put it in the freezer. Check it at the end of the day. Check it at the end of a week. What does the rag feel like?

At the end of the day, the rag will feel stiff. The water in the wet rag will have changed to ice. At the end of the week, the rag will feel soft and not wet. The ice will have changed to frost. The frost stays inside the freezer.

Will the ice cubes sink?

You will need: 3 ice cubes, a deep dish, and water.

Fill the dish with water. Place the three ice cubes in water.

Do the ice cubes sink? Do they stay at the top?

The three ice cubes do not sink. They stay at the top. When water changes to ice, it takes up more space. This makes the ice lighter than water.

What can ice do to glass?

You will need: a glass bottle that is not needed anymore, a cap for the bottle, a bag, and water.

Fill the bottle to the top with water. Put the cap on. Put the bottle in the bag. Put the bag in the freezer for a day. Then take out the bag and look at the bottle. Don't take the bottle from the bag.

The glass has many cracks. The water in the glass changed to ice. Since ice takes up more space than water, the glass cracked. The bottle did not have space for all the ice.

Will the clay sink?

You will need: clay, a deep dish, and water.
Fill the dish with water. Press the clay into a lump. Put the lump of clay into the water. Then make the clay flat and thin. Put it back in the water. What does the clay do in the water?

The lump of clay sinks. The flat, thin clay stays at the top. The lump of clay takes up less space in the water. There is less water to keep it up. The flat, thin clay takes up more space in the water. There is more water to keep it at the top.

Study Guide

ay words	*ee* words	new study words
maybe	need	lighter
day	see	bottle
way	seem	out
stay	three	
clay	feel	
	freezer	
	week	
	deep	
	keep	

Language Concept: fraction (½)

Fun and Games with Water and Ice

Focus: *ea, oa*

Jokes

What do you get when you toss a green rock into the Red Sea?
A wet rock.

What water can't freeze?
Hot water.

Should you tell a joke while you're ice skating?
No, the ice would crack up.

Play a Trick

Get a clear, clean glass. Fill it with water. Lay a cloth over the glass. Say to your pal, "I shall drink the water in this glass, but I will not take off the cloth to do it."

Wave your hand over the glass. Say, "The water will not be in the glass."

But your pal will say, "The water is still there."
Let your pal take off the cloth to check. Pick up the glass and drink the water. You did the trick! You drank the water that was under the cloth. *You* didn't take off the cloth!

The Floating Needle
Fill a glass with water. Get a needle and paper. Give your pal just the needle. Ask your pal if she can make the needle float. The needle will sink.

Take the paper. Place it in the water. Put the needle on the paper. The needle will stay on top. The needle floats on the paper as if it were on a boat.

Making 2 Dimes from 1

Fill a glass ⅔ full with water. Drop in a dime. Lay a plate on top of the glass. Flip the glass over. Don't spill the water!

Stand up and look into the glass. You will see 2 dimes. One dime will be near the base. One dime will seem to be floating.

Making a Mask

Cut paper into strips. In a pan, make a thick paste with flour and water. Soak the strips of paper in the paste. Get a deep dish.

Put the strips of paper on the deep dish. Make the layers thick. Shape it like a face. The next day take the mask off the dish.

More Jokes, Please

Why do elephants float on their backs?
To keep their sneakers from getting wet.

Why did the elephants have to leave the swim club?
They couldn't keep their trunks up.

Stringing Ice

Fill a glass ⅔ full with water. Drop in an ice cube. Take a thick string three inches long. Wet the end of the string. Lay it on the floating ice. Shake a little salt on the spot where the string is on the ice. Lift the ice up with the string.

Make a Nice Cold Snack

Make some punch that you like. Get an ice cube tray. Fill the tray with punch. Put the tray in the freezer. The next day, you will have ice pops for a snack on a hot day.

Pea Plants

The peas we eat are seeds. Buy some fresh peas. Take the peas from the pod. Place soft paper in a dish. Set the peas on it. Just wet the paper with water. Add water each day to keep the peas wet. In a week the peas will change. Then you can plant them in a pot.

More Jokes to Read

What is full of holes, yet keeps water?
A sponge.

What can run, but can't jog?
Water.

What could you add to a tub of water to make it lighter?
Holes.

When will a net keep water?
When the water is ice.

Study Guide

ea words	*oa* words	new study words
sea	float	should
clear	soak	would
clean	boat	needle
near		paper
please		flour
sneaker		elephant
leave		could
peas		salt
eat		
each		
read		

A Land of Ice and Snow

Focus: *ai, ow, ue*

Antarctica is a very big place. Look at the map. See where Antarctica is? There is a lot of ice and snow on the land. The ice can be more than a mile thick. There is no place as cold as Antarctica. Very little of the ice and snow melts. The land by the coast would be under water if a lot of the ice and snow were to melt.

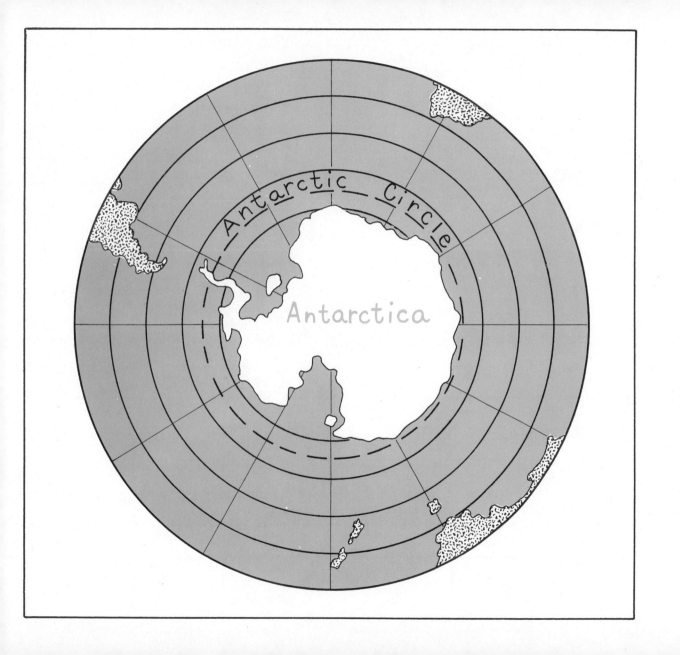

The sun doesn't set for six months. Then there is no sunshine for the next six months. It is very cold. It never warms up. There is very little rain at Antarctica. But very strong winds blow there. The coast of Antarctica is just ice. The ice is well packed. It is as strong as steel.

Sometimes this pack ice splits. It floats into the seas. These chunks of floating ice are icebergs. It is true that an iceberg can be bigger than a ship.

Icebergs can float over 1,000 miles away.

Much of an iceberg is under water. Some ships sail to see where the icebergs are floating. It is their job to tell ships where it is safe. Ships can get crushed by the icebergs.

We think of ice as being clear and snow as being white. But at Antarctica, the ice and snow sometimes seem to have color. The ice can look like it is blue, green, or yellow.

It's so cold that the only living things live by the coast. Near the coast, there are rocks that stick up from the ice. Some low moss grows on these rocks. Some bugs live here, too.

Very little plants live in the water. They are too little to see. Krill eat these plants. Krill are little and look like shrimp. Clams, squid, and fish live in the sea. They feed on the krill. Seals, gulls, and penguins live on the ice sheets at the coast. They eat the clams, squid, fish, and krill.

There is pack ice along the coast. Under this ice there is water, not land. Seals stay on this floating pack ice. They hunt in the waters for things to eat. Seals can dive very deep. Their shape helps them to swim well. Thick fat keeps the seals warm.

Penguins live only at Antarctica. Some can be 15 inches big. Some can be as big as 4 feet. Penguins live on floating ice like the seals. They slide off the ice to jump into the water.

When the bigger penguins lay their eggs, they have no nest. The male places the egg on his feet. A flap of skin covers the egg and keeps it warm. It takes nine weeks for the egg to hatch.

Huge whales come to Antarctica once a year. Their strong tails help them to swim. The blue whale is the biggest living thing. Whales eat huge meals of krill each day. They eat the krill as they drink water.

For many years only seal hunters sailed to Antarctica. They didn't come onto the land.

It was over 150 years ago that men went on the land. Since then many teams of men have sailed and flown to Antarctica.

Long ago, a plane landed on Antarctica. A team of men from the plane set up camp. The men wanted to see what it was like there.

After a while, more men and some women went to Antarctica to get facts. Today, there are men and women from all over who work in Antarctica.

A while ago, teams from all over the world went to Antarctica to work for a year as one big team. Today, the teams still help each other to get facts. But no one stays in Antarctica to live.

There is no place anywhere like Antarctica.

Study Guide

ūe words	*āi* words	*ōw* words	new study words
true	rain	snow	Antarctica
blue	sail	blow	never
	tail	yellow	iceberg
		low	color
		grow	penguin
		flown	cover
			women
			world

Language Concept: paragraph indenting

Diana Nyad

Focus: *īe, ew,* schwa *a*

When Diana Nyad was little, she lived in a warm place near the water. So, she swam a lot. From the time she was ten, she wanted to be the best swimmer in the world. So Diana made a plan.

Before school, she would swim from 5:30–7:30. This was before the sun came up. Diana was alone in the water. After school, Diana did not play much. She swam until it was time to eat. By the time Diana was 12, she was swimming every chance she had. Diana wanted to swim more than anything.

Diana tried to swim as much as she could. She had a new plan. She wanted to win the Olympic swimming race. The Olympics have worldwide races. Swimmers come from many places in the world to race. If Diana could win the Olympics, she would be the best swimmer in the world!

Diana needed a coach to help her train. The coach felt Diana could be an Olympic swimmer. Diana did just what her coach said.

Diana once swam when she had a bad cold. She got so sick that she had to lie in bed for three months. When she was feeling well, she went back to swimming. But she could not swim as fast as before. She had to give up going to the Olympics! This made Diana very sad.

Diana did not quit swimming. She made a new plan. She would be a long-distance swimmer. This means swimming for a very, very long time. A swimmer must be very strong. Long-distance races sometimes last from sunrise to sunset. Sometimes these races can be longer!

When Diana swims a long distance, a boat goes along with her. Diana can't see the crew in the boat. She can just see the boat. The crew in the boat feeds Diana. They give her broth many times while she is swimming. Diana needs to be fed to keep her strength.

When Diana was 24 she wanted to swim across a very big lake. She planned to take a little rest once she got across. Then she would swim back.

When Diana made the swim, the water in the lake was very cold. Just as she got into the water, the wind picked up. Diana had to swim with huge waves pushing at her. The waves grew bigger and bigger. She got very cold.

At last, Diana got across the lake. She had swum 32 miles! She had very little rest. Then she jumped back into the cold water. But the waves were just as big as before. Diana tried and tried. At last, she could no longer keep swimming. The crew lifted her onto the boat.

Diana felt very weak and tired. Men from the news asked her what the long swim was like. Diana said she had felt a little upset before the long swim. She had felt very alone while swimming in the lake. She couldn't hear anything but the splashing of the water on her swim cap. Her swimming glasses had fogged up. She couldn't see anything.

But she would not give up her plan. The next year, she tried once more and made it!

When Diana was 25, she tried to swim in the New York waters. That was a swim of 28 miles. When she swam, it was raining and the tide was pushing her back. It grew late. Big ships and tugboats seemed to come at her. She couldn't make it to the end. Diana had to stop swimming. Just a few New Yorkers had come to see her swim.

But Diana did not quit. She planned to go back to New York. This time, she would not get into the water at the same place. She planned to let the tide help her. The tide could push her faster. When Diana went back to swim, the tide didn't help her at all for a while. Then her plan worked! The tide changed. She was swimming with the tide.

This time, many New Yorkers came and cheered for Diana. It grew late. Diana was having a bad time. She had to swim past lots of junk in the water. Her swimming glasses filled with mud from the water. But more New Yorkers kept coming to the water yelling, "Keep on, Diana. You can make it!" Diana did not feel alone this time. On and on she swam.

At last, Diana got to the end. Everyone cheered. She had swum the waters faster than anyone! Diana said she had felt pain, and she had felt cold. The swim had taken a very long time. Yet she had made it. The time and work she had spent in training had paid off. Her plan had worked. She was a world champ!

Diana's coach said Diana is the best swimmer he had ever coached. She is a champ. She is the world's best long-distance swimmer. Winners are those who don't give up.

Study Guide

īe words	*ēw* words	schwa *ā* words	new study words
tried	new	a	Diana Nyad
lie	crew	alone	before
	few	along	until
	grew	across	Olympics
			distance
			New York
			ever

Language Concept: time (5:30–7:30)

Eric and Beth Heiden

Focus: single long vowels

What's it like to be a world champ? Eric and Beth Heiden could tell you. Both are world champs at speed skating. But, not everyone can be a champ. It takes much time, training, and work. Eric and Beth have been skating for most of their lives. Beth and Eric never give up.

When Eric and Beth were little, they lived by a lake. For many months, the lake was ice. Their grandma, grandpa, mom, and dad were fine skaters. Eric had on skates when he was just two. Once he could skate by himself, he didn't want to get off the ice. Beth went everywhere with Eric and his pals. So, she spent much time on the ice, too.

Their mom and dad liked skating, swimming, running, biking, and hiking. Their mom was a gym teacher. Their dad was a doctor for runners, boxers, and swimmers. Both were glad that Eric and Beth liked skating so much. Eric and Beth went to a skating club. They liked to race more than dance on skates. They liked to go fast on the ice. So they switched to a speed skating club.

Speed skating is a race in a rink. A speed skating race is a "meet." Two skaters race at one time. They keep skating for a mile, sometimes more. Then the clock stops. It tells the time they skated. Sometimes more than ten skaters will be in a meet. After a few years, Eric and Beth won prizes at speed skating races.

When Eric was 13 and Beth was 12, Dianne Holum came to coach their club. She was a speed skating champ. Eric and Beth needed training to do their best on the ice. Training was work. They would get tired. Their legs would be in pain. Sometimes Eric felt like quitting. Beth kept him going. She helped him stick with the training.

Races were held for three months. Their mom and dad drove them to the races and stayed to cheer. The rest of the year was for training. When the ice melted, they still had to keep in shape. So they trained off the ice, too. Eric and Beth spent much time running and biking. Their mom and dad set up a gym in their home.

Eric and Beth did their homework before the races. This was a strict rule in their home. Beth and Eric never missed a race. Yet they got top grades. Their mom and dad did not push them to race and win prizes. What Eric and Beth wanted to do the most was to race. Dianne helped them skate with skill and speed.

When Beth and Eric were older, they were taking long trips. They raced in world meets. They won many races. In some races, their skating was faster than anyone had seen.

Dianne had trained them for over five years. In June of 1979, Eric and Beth were set for training camp. They packed their bikes and skates. These skates had three wheels and no blades. This kind of skate was used off the ice. This time their training was for the best race ever, the one at the 1980 World Olympics.

At the Olympic games, Eric and Beth wanted to do as well as they could. They dressed in gold. The skaters got set to step into the rink. Beth glided onto the ice with much grace. She was in four races and did well. She won a third place medal. Eric was in five races. He won each of the five races. No one had ever won five gold medals in the Olympics.

Some say Eric is the best skater in the world. Eric stepped up to get his gold medals. Wild cheers filled the rink! The long training had paid off. He was glad Beth had never let him quit. His medals were not just for him. They were Beth's and his dad's and mom's, and Dianne Holum's, too. One doesn't become a world champ alone.

Study Guide

single long vowels	new study words
be	Eric Heiden
both	grandma
most	gym
he	doctor
so	won
she	Dianne Holum
go	third
older	medal
no	
kind	
gold	
wild	

Teaching Guide

THE BOOKS

This early reading program is designed to help children become fluent, independent, lifelong readers. The more children read, the better readers they become, both in their schoolwork and at home on their own. This program consists of six sets of six books each that cover 1st- through 3rd-grade reading levels. The books offer a variety of factual and fictional stories, with an underlying theme for each of the six sets.

The reading vocabulary is linguistically controlled and contains all 220 words of the Dolch Basic Word List. These words are widely viewed as the basic vocabulary essential to fluent reading.

New words are introduced in a careful sequence from book to book and from set to set. The stories are written to increase reading comprehension, and many involve the children as active participants. All stories build on the speaking vocabulary of the child so that even a preschooler, with beginning reading skills, will enjoy the stories.

THE CHILDREN

Whether a child's progress in reading is advanced, average, or delayed, all children need reading practice as they master a widening vocabulary, acquire language skills, and attain fluency. Children can en-

joy these books whether at home with parents, in school with the classroom teacher or remedial specialist, or in public and school libraries with the librarians.

THE METHOD

The LEARN TO READ books offer a carefully structured and tested approach to reading. Emphasis is on the use of the *sound* names of letters rather than the traditional *alphabet* names. For example, when you say the word *fun*, you hear that it starts with a /f/ sound. That is the sound name of the letter; you hear only the pure consonant, not a vowel sound attached to the consonant. The alphabet name /ef/ has a completely different sound. Knowing the sound names of the letters is *the* most important tool in becoming a good reader.

Each of these 36 books has its own focus, whether it be the introduction of a certain sound or a new group of structurally related words. In Book 1 of Set I, the focus is short *a*, as in *man*. In Book 2 it is short *i*, as in *dig*, and so on. At the end of each book is a study guide to the new words introduced in that particular book. This guide will have word lists: for the new vocabulary relating to the focus of that book and for the phonetically irregular words, the so-called "study," or "sight," words. The child should read these lists before beginning to read the story.

To help the child read the new vocabulary words, you should first explain the specific focus of the book. Then, proceed to introduce the new vocabulary by the method outlined below for each set.

Set I introduces the phonetically regular words with short vowel sounds. Here, as in the other sets, the new words should be approached as they are naturally spoken. For example, most phonics programs instruct the child to read the word *cat* as *c + at.* Yet *cat* is spoken as *ca + t.* This program's approach is to use a child's natural speech patterns and to teach words the way a child reads them, from left to right.

Thus, to help a child sound out a specific word, cover the word to expose only the initial consonant sound(s) and the vowel sound. For example, with the word *man*, once the child has pronounced the main part *ma* as a unit, you can then reveal the final sound in the word:

ma + n = man   tha + t = that

This method may be used throughout Set I.

Books in **Set II** focus on consonant blends, such as *st* or *dr*, and the inflectional endings *ing*, *ed*, and *er.* Consonant blends should be taught on the basis of the same blending process used in Set I:

la + st = last   dro + p = drop

To teach inflectional endings, have the child read the root (or base) word first, then expose the inflectional endings:

bring + ing = bringing
stop + ping = stopping

Set III focuses on words that have long vowels and end in silent *e.* Tell the child that the final *e* remains silent, yet functions to make the preceding vowel say its alphabet name:

ca + ne = cane   smi + le = smile

Set IV introduces soft sounds for consonants *c* and *g*, long vowel sounds other than those ending in silent *e*, and the schwa, or weak *a*, sound in words like *alone.* To help the child understand hard and soft consonant sounds, review familiar words with hard *c* and *g*, such as *can, cab, cape,* and *get, game, gate.* Then explain that *c* and *g* make a soft sound /s/ and /j/, respectively, in words like *cent, ice, gem,* and *age.*

Introduce the double long vowel sounds presented in this set by showing the child that when two vowels come together, usually the first one says its alphabet name and the second one is silent:

bōat fēet tīe blūe māin

In Book 5 of this set, point out to the child that many words beginning with *a* have a weakened sound as in *alone, along, across.*

In Book 6, note that sometimes a single vowel can make a long vowel sound as in *child, kind,* and *cold.*

Set V focuses on variant vowel sounds: that is, vowel sounds that are neither long nor short. To help the child understand variant vowels, explain that sometimes consonants like *r, l, y,* or *w*, will control the vowel sound:

car ball boy cow saw

Sometimes, two vowels will work together to make a new sound as with *oo, oi,* and *au*:

book oil tool fault

Set VI presents a variety of advanced word structures. Book I introduces two-syllable words with double consonants. Explain to the child how to divide these words between the double consonants and then read each syllable as a simple unit:

but ton   yel low

Book 1 also introduces the irregular vowels *ea* that make a short *e* sound (h*ea*d) and the construction *o*—silent *e* that makes a short *u* sound (c*ome*).

Book 2 focuses on *y* as a vowel with a long *e* sound when it comes at the end of multi-syllable words. Review familiar words with consonant *y*, such as *yes, yarn, year*. Explain to the child that *y* can sometimes be a consonant and sometimes a vowel. At the end of some words, *y* makes the sound of long *e*:

sun ny   han dy   cit y

Book 2 also introduces the irregular vowels *ie* that make a long *e* sound (ch*ie*f) and the construction *ear* that makes a variant /er/ sound (b*ear*, *ear* th).

Book 3 introduces *y* as a vowel with a long *i* sound when it comes at the end of one-syllable words such as *by, cry,* and *fly*. Two-syllable words ending with *le* are also introduced. Explain that the final syllable has a schwa or weakened vowel sound:

ta ble   bot tle

Book 4 presents silent consonants. Review which letters are consonants and which are vowels. Explain that sometimes the consonants *b, d, g, h, k, l, w* are silent in some words:

We*d*nesday ni*gh*t *h*our *k*now wa*l* k *w*rite com*b* si*g*n

Show the words to the child, say them, and ask the child to identify the silent consonants.

Books 5 and 6 focus on prefixes and suffixes. Explain to the child that a prefix is a syllable added to the beginning of a word that changes its meaning. Knowing the meaning of the prefixes often helps in understanding the meaning of the new word:

un- not	*dis*- not, opposite of
re- again	*ex*- out of
pro- before, forward, favoring	*in*- in, into, not

A suffix is a syllable added to the end of a word to change its meaning. As with prefixes, it helps to know the meaning of the suffixes:

-ful full of	*-tion* act or process
-ly in the manner of	*-ness* state of being
-ment state of, act of	

Be sure children realize they will not *always* be able to determine the meaning of the new word simply by knowing the prefix or suffix meaning. For example, those words with Greek or Latin roots will not be familiar to them, but have been included in these books in order to reinforce the reading of multi-syllable words

Study Words, which are listed separately from the new vocabulary words in each study guide, are words that do not follow a regular spelling pattern. To introduce these study words, first you, and then the child, should use each one in a sentence to make sure the child knows it on a spoken level. Help the child recognize which sounds are irregular. For example, the study word *said* has the regular consonant sounds /s/ and /d/. It is only the vowel sound /ĕ/ which has the irregular spelling of *ai*.

Comprehension is, of course, essential to the development of a successful reader. Discuss each story after it is read. You may find that follow-up activities, such as making a picture of an element from the story, thinking up new characters for the story, making up a play from the story and getting friends to help act it out, etc., will add further to the pleasure and comprehension of each book. While the books are intended to be presented in sequence, the re-reading of books already presented should be encouraged. When children enjoy reading and are successful, their confidence inspires them to want to read more.